The Shipwrecked Sailor

A TALE FROM EGYPT

Retold by Suzanne I. Barchers
Illustrated by Shelly Hehenberger

RED
CHAIR
·PRESS·

Please visit our website at **www.redchairpress.com**.
Find a free catalog of all our high-quality products for young readers.

For a free activity page for this story, go to
www.redchairpress.com and look for Free Activities.

The Shipwrecked Sailor

Publisher's Cataloging-In-Publication Data
(Prepared by The Donohue Group, Inc.)

Barchers, Suzanne I.
    The Shipwrecked Sailor: a tale from Egypt / retold by Suzanne I. Barchers ;
illustrated by Shelly Hehenberger.

    pages : illustrations ; cm. -- (Tales of honor)

    Summary: Sadiki fears the worst when he is tossed from his ship in a storm. But a
chance encounter with a serpent changes his life and that of the Pharaoh.
    Interest age level: 006-009.
    Issued also as an ebook.
    ISBN: 978-1-939656-86-5 (library binding)
    ISBN: 978-1-939656-87-2 (paperback)

    1. Sailors--Juvenile fiction. 2. Serpents--Juvenile fiction. 3. Kings and rulers--Juvenile
fiction. 4. Folklore--Egypt. 5. Sailors--Fiction. 6. Snakes--Fiction. 7. Kings, queens,
rulers, etc.--Fiction. 8. Folklore--Egypt. 9. Electronic books. I. Hehenberger, Shelly.
II. Title. III. Series: Barchers, Suzanne. Tales of honor.

PZ8.1.B37 Sh 2015
398.2/73/0932   2014944306

This series first published by:
Red Chair Press LLC   PO Box 333   South Egremont, MA 01258-0333

Printed in the United States of America

WZ1114   1 2 3 4 5 18 17 16 15 14

Once there was a sailor, called Sadiki, who
traveled far and wide. He loved the journeys
and the challenge of the sea. But there was one
journey that was so **perilous**, that he scarcely
believed what happened—or that he survived.
This is his story.

Sadiki had joined a crew of 150 sailors, the best group of sailors that Egypt had to offer. It was said that their hearts had more understanding than the hearts of lions. They were so skilled that they could look into the sky and tell when a **tempest** was coming. Indeed, they could tell when a squall was going to rise up before they felt a single breeze.

The sailors were set to sail to the copper
mines of **Pharaoh**. But fate changed the course
of their journey. A vicious storm overtook
them, one that even those fine sailors had not
foreseen. The men were helpless.

The wind blew so hard that a 12-foot wave **capsized** the ship. Sadiki seized a plank that was hurtling past and held on tightly. The seas raged, and the sailor thought that all was lost. Still, he hung on to the plank with all his strength.

Finally, a great wave cast Sadiki upon an island. Exhausted, he slept in a hollow in a **thicket**, hugging the shade. After three days, hunger pangs forced Sadiki to search for something to eat.

Imagine his delight when he found figs, grapes, and large berries of all kinds! There were gourds, melons, and pumpkins as large as barrels. Fish and waterfowl swam nearby, almost as if they were waiting to be caught.

It seemed that every food of any sort grew on the island. After he had eaten his fill, he decided to honor the gods that brought him safely to this abundant land. He dug a hole in the ground and gathered wood for a fire. Soon his burnt offering was complete.

Suddenly, Sadiki heard what sounded like thunder. The earth quaked and the trees rocked, and he thought a great wave must have hit the shore. Looking around, he saw a serpent gliding toward him. It was 45 feet long and covered with scales of gold. Its head was three feet long, and the two ridges over its eyes were of pure **lapis lazuli**.

The sailor dropped flat on the ground. The serpent coiled its whole length and said, "Who brought you here? If you don't tell me, you'll soon learn what it is like to burn like fire and become invisible!"

Sadiki trembled, speechless.

The serpent picked up the sailor with his mouth. To the sailor's surprise, the serpent held him gently. He carried Sadiki to his lair, setting him down by a rock. Then he asked again: "Who brought you here, oh miserable one? Who brought you to this island in the sea?"

Finding his voice, the sailor told his story. "I was traveling to the mines for the Pharaoh, part of a crew of 150 fine sailors. A gale rose before we could make land. A mighty wave capsized the ship. If I hadn't seized a plank of wood, I'd have perished with the crew. The sea brought me to this island, and here I am by your side!"

"Have no fear, my friend," the serpent said. "Your life has been spared and you have been brought here where there is food of every kind. This is what will happen. You will pass the time comfortably on this island. After four months, a ship shall arrive. It will bring sailors of your **acquaintance**, and you shall go home to your country. Indeed, you will die an old man in your native land."

The grateful Sadiki asked, "But what of you? How did you come to be on this island?"

The sailor rested against the rock as the serpent told its story.

"I used to live on this island with my family and all my children. Together, we numbered 75, living happily in this land of plenty. One day, a star fell from above, bringing fire with it. I was not with my family, so I escaped the fire. But I nearly died of grief. I buried my entire family together."

The serpent continued, "You, my friend, have lost much. But if you are faithful and of good heart, you will live to see your own house and country. You will kiss your wife and embrace your children. That is the most beautiful thing of all."

Sadiki threw himself on the ground in front of the serpent. "I will tell Pharaoh about your greatness. I will tell him all you have lost, and how you still have compassion. I will have him bring you spices, incense, and oils in gratitude for your kindness. I will build burnt offerings in your honor. I will send you boats laden with riches. Even though you are far away, you will be treated as a great god who is good to man."

The serpent smiled at the sailor and
spoke quietly.

"Egypt does not have a great store of **myrrh** or
of incense. Look around. I have everything I
could ever want growing here on this island."

The serpent paused for a moment before continuing. "Truly, once you depart, you will never return. This island will disappear into the distant waves."

As the serpent predicted, one day a ship could be seen approaching the island. Sadiki climbed to the top of a tree and recognized some of the sailors. He found the serpent and told it of the ship's arrival.

"Yes, I knew that the ship would appear one day," the serpent said. "You will have a safe journey home. I ask one favor, that you will hold me in high regard after your return. This is all that I ask."

The sailor threw himself on the ground, thanking the serpent.

The serpent gave the sailor enough gifts to fill the ship's hold: myrrh, spices, incense, **antimony**, and more. When Sadiki had loaded everything in the ship, he returned to thank the serpent. Then he had the men of the ship give their thanksgiving to the lord of the island.

While the men set sail for home, the
shipwrecked sailor watched the island
fade away into the distance.

After two months, the sailor was home again. He brought his many treasures to Pharaoh, telling him all that had happened on his journey. In front of all the nobles of the country, the Pharaoh praised Sadiki for his courage and devotion. Then Pharaoh appointed Sadiki to be his bodyguard, a most **exalted** position.

Now, as promised, Sadiki could spend his
days with his wife and children. He was
content with his life on land, grateful to be
a bodyguard to the Pharaoh. He would tell
his story of the honorable serpent to all who
would listen.

And on days when the thunder rumbled, he could not help himself. Sadiki would turn, hoping to see his old friend gliding toward him.

acquaintance: something or someone familiar

antimony: a chemical element, silver in appearance, used for cosmetics in ancient Egypt

capsized: overturned in water

exalted: held in high esteem

lapis lazuli: a bright blue stone; the color or stone is used for decoration

myrrh: a tree gum or resin with a pleasing odor found in the Middle East

perilous: full of danger or risk

Pharaoh: a king in ancient Egypt

tempest: a violent, windy storm

thicket: dense brush

WHAT DO YOU THINK?

Question 1: The serpent said that the island will disappear into the waves once the sailor leaves. Do you think the serpent means that the island will sink and disappear forever? Or do you think it could not be found again?

Question 2: If you were Sadiki, would you want to be a bodyguard or would you want to return to the sea? Explain your choice.

Question 3: Do you think the sailor should have been allowed to keep some of the treasure? Justify your choice.

Question 4: If you heard the sailor tell this story, would you believe it? Why or why not?

About Ancient Egypt

Egypt is home to one of the oldest civilizations on Earth. For thousands of years Egypt was defined by flow of the Nile River. Lower Egypt was the region where the Nile formed many branches to the sea. Upper Egypt was the southern region near Nubia and the Kush. These two distinct kingdoms are thought to have been united by Menes (Ma'nij) around 3,000 BC, becoming the first pharaoh or king of Dynasty 1. The pharaohs often introduced the worship of new gods or deities which were thought to be good luck.

About the Author

After fifteen years as a teacher, Suzanne Barchers began a career in writing and publishing. She has written over 100 children's books. She previously held editorial roles at Weekly Reader and LeapFrog and is on the PBS Kids Media Advisory Board. Suzanne also plays the flute professionally – and for fun – from her home in Stanford, CA.

About the Illustrator

Shelly Hehenberger has been illustrating children's books since 1996. She has a degree in Graphic Design from Indiana University, and a Master of Fine Arts degree in painting from the University of Cincinnati. She is also an art teacher and abstract painter. Shelly currently lives near Chapel Hill, NC, with her husband and teenage daughter. The illustrations in this book were created using hand-painted textures and patterns that have been collaged digitally.